STOP! GO! WORD BIRD

by Jane Belk Moncure
illustrated by Linda Sommers Hohag

THE CHILD'S WORLD
MANKATO, MN 56001

Library of Congress Cataloging in Publication Data

Moncure, Jane Belk.
  Stop! Go! Word Bird.

  (Her Word Birds for early birds)
  SUMMARY: Uses a very simple vocabulary to follow
Word Bird and his family's trip by car to their
mountain-top retreat.
  [1. Travel—Fiction] I. Hohag, Linda Sommers.
II. Title. III. Series.

PZ7.M739St   [E]   80-16273
ISBN 0-89565-160-2 -1991 Edition

Go.

Stop sign.
Stop.

Go.

Red light. Stop.

Green light. Go.

Stop, car. Stop.

Go, train, go.

Go, motorcycle, go.

Go, car.
Go fast.

Go down.

Stop.

Go slow.

Go, fire engine.
Go fast.

Go, ambulance.
Go fast.

17

Go, car.
Turn right.

Go, car.
Turn left.

Stop.

Wait.

Slow down.

Go up and around.

Slow down.

Bump. Bump.

Stop. Park.

Look. Listen. Wait.

Hippety-hop
to the top.

Home. Home.
Hippety-hop.

Can you read these words with  Word Bird?

go

stop sign

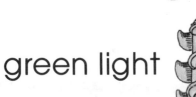

car

red light

green light

motorcycle

train

fire engine

 ambulance

up ⬆ down ⬇

right ➡ left ⬅

slow fast

bump  hippety-hop

top  home

You can read Word Bird's safety signs.

STOP!
LOOK!
LISTEN!
WAIT!
before you
cross the street.